# Frog and Together

ARNOLD LOBEL

I CAN READ

MAMMOTH

For Barbara Dicks

First published in Great Britain 1973
by World's Work Ltd
Published 1992 by Mammoth
an imprint of Mandarin Paperbacks
Michelin House, 81 Fulham Road, London SW3 6RB

Mandarin is an imprint of the Octopus Publishing Group,
a division of Reed International Books Ltd

Copyright © 1971, 1972 Arnold Lobel

'I Can Read' is a registered
trademark in the USA of Harper Collins

A portion of this book previously appeared in *Woman's Day*

ISBN 0 7497 1209 0

A CIP catalogue record for this title
is available from the British Library

Printed in Great Britain
by Scotprint Ltd., Musselburgh

# Contents

## A List

One morning Toad sat in bed.

"I have many things to do," he said.

"I will write them

all down on a list

so that I can remember them."

Toad wrote on a piece of paper:

A List of things to do today

Then he wrote:

Wake up

"I have done that," said Toad,

and he crossed out:

~~Wake up~~

Then Toad wrote other things
on the paper.

A List
of things to do
today

~~Wake up~~

Eat Breakfast

Get Dressed

Go to Frog's House

Take walk with Frog

Eat lunch

Take nap

Play games with Frog

Eat Supper

Go To Sleep

"There," said Toad.

"Now my day

is all written down."

He got out of bed

and had something to eat.

Then Toad crossed out:

~~Eat Breakfast~~

Toad took his clothes

out of the cupboard

and put them on.

Then he crossed out:

~~Get Dressed~~

Toad put the list in his pocket.

He opened the door

and walked out into the morning.

Soon Toad was at Frog's front door.

He took the list from his pocket

and crossed out:

~~Go to Frog's House~~

Toad knocked at the door.

"Hello," said Frog.

"Look at my list

of things to do,"

said Toad.

"Oh," said Frog,

"that is very nice."

Toad said, "My list tells me

that we will go

for a walk."

"All right," said Frog.

"I am ready."

Frog and Toad

went on a long walk.

Then Toad took the list

from his pocket again.

He crossed out:

~~Take walk with Frog~~

Just then there was a strong wind.

It blew the list

out of Toad's hand.

The list blew high up

into the air.

"Help!" cried Toad.

"My list is blowing away.

What will I do without my list?"

13

"Hurry!" said Frog.

"We will run and catch it."

"No!" shouted Toad.

"I cannot do that."

"Why not?" asked Frog.

"Because," wailed Toad,

"running after my list

is not one of the things

that I wrote

on my list of things to do!"

14

Frog ran after the list.

He ran over hills and swamps,

but the list blew on and on.

At last Frog came back to Toad.

"I am sorry," gasped Frog,

"but I could not catch

your list."

"Blah," said Toad.

"I cannot remember any of the things
that were on my list of things to do.
I will just have to sit here
and do nothing," said Toad.
Toad sat and did nothing.
Frog sat with him.

After a long time Frog said,
"Toad, it is getting dark.
We should be going to sleep now."

"Go to sleep!" shouted Toad.

"That was the last thing on my list!"

Toad wrote on the ground

with a stick: Go to sleep

Then he crossed out:

~~Go to sleep~~

"There," said Toad.

"Now my day

is all crossed out!"

"I am glad,"

said Frog.

Then Frog and Toad

went to sleep.

## The Garden

Frog was in his garden.

Toad came walking by.

"What a fine garden

you have, Frog," he said.

"Yes," said Frog. "It is very nice,

but it was hard work."

"I wish I had a garden," said Toad.

"Here are some flower seeds.

Plant them in the ground," said Frog,

"and soon you will have a garden."

"How soon?" asked Toad.

"Quite soon," said Frog.

19

Toad ran home.

He planted the flower seeds.

"Now seeds," said Toad,

"start growing."

Toad walked up and down

a few times.

The seeds did not start to grow.

Toad put his head

close to the ground

and said loudly,

"Now seeds, start growing!"

Toad looked at the ground again.

The seeds did not start to grow.

Toad put his head

very close to the ground and shouted,

"NOW SEEDS, START GROWING!"

Frog came running up the path.

"What is all this noise?" he asked.

"My seeds will not grow," said Toad.

"You are shouting too much,"

said Frog. "These poor seeds

are afraid to grow."

"My seeds are afraid to grow?"

asked Toad.

"Of course," said Frog.

"Leave them alone for a few days.

Let the sun shine on them,

let the rain fall on them.

Soon your seeds will start to grow."

That night

Toad looked out of his window.

"Bother!" said Toad.

"My seeds have not

started to grow.

They must be afraid of the dark."

Toad went out to his garden

with some candles.

"I will read the seeds a story,"

said Toad.

"Then they will not be afraid."

Toad read a long story

to his seeds.

All the next day
Toad sang songs
to his seeds.

And all the next day
Toad read poems
to his seeds.

And all the next day
Toad played music
for his seeds.

Toad looked at the ground.

The seeds still did not

start to grow.

"What shall I do?" cried Toad.

"These must be

the most frightened seeds

in the whole world!"

Then Toad felt very tired,

and he fell asleep.

"Toad, Toad, wake up," said Frog.

"Look at your garden!"

Toad looked at his garden.

Little green plants were coming up
out of the ground.

28

"At last," shouted Toad,
"my seeds have stopped
being afraid to grow!"
"And now you will have
a nice garden too," said Frog.
"Yes," said Toad,
"but you were right, Frog.
It was very hard work."

## Cookies

Toad baked some cookies.

"These cookies smell very good,"

said Toad.

He ate one.

"And they taste even better," he said.

Toad ran to Frog's house.

"Frog, Frog," cried Toad,

"taste these cookies

that I have made."

Frog ate one of the cookies.

"These are the best cookies

I have ever eaten!" said Frog.

Frog and Toad ate many cookies,
one after another.

"You know, Toad," said Frog,
with his mouth full,
"I think we should stop eating.
We will soon be sick."

"You are right," said Toad.

"Let us eat one last cookie,

and then we will stop."

Frog and Toad ate

one last cookie.

There were many cookies

left in the bowl.

"Frog," said Toad,

"let us eat one very last cookie,

and then we will stop."

Frog and Toad

ate one very last cookie.

"We must stop eating!" cried Toad

as he ate another.

"Yes," said Frog,

reaching for a cookie

"we need will power."

"What is will power?" asked Toad.

"Will power is trying hard

*not* to do something

that you really want to do,"

said Frog.

"You mean like trying *not*

to eat all of these cookies?"

asked Toad.

"Right," said Frog.

Frog put the cookies in a box.

"There," he said.

"Now we will not eat
any more cookies."

"But we can open the box,"
said Toad.

"That is true," said Frog.

Frog tied some string
round the box.
"There," he said.
"Now we will not eat
any more cookies."
"But we can cut the string
and open the box," said Toad.
"That is true," said Frog.

Frog got a ladder.

He put the box up on a high shelf.

"There," said Frog.

"Now we will not eat

any more cookies."

"But we can climb the ladder

and take the box

down from the shelf

and cut the string

and open the box,"

said Toad.

"That is true," said Frog.

Frog climbed the ladder

and took the box

down from the shelf.

He cut the string

and opened the box.

Frog took the box outside.

He shouted in a loud voice,

"HEY BIRDS,

HERE ARE COOKIES!"

Birds came from everywhere.

They picked up all the cookies

in their beaks and flew away.

"Now we have no more cookies to eat,"

said Toad sadly.

"Not even one."

"Yes," said Frog,

"but we have lots and lots

of will power."

"You may keep it all, Frog,"

said Toad.

"I am going home now

to bake a cake."

## Dragons and Giants

Frog and Toad

were reading a book together.

"The people in this book

are brave," said Toad.

"They fight dragons and giants,

and they are never afraid."

"I wonder if we are brave,"

said Frog.

Frog and Toad looked into a mirror.

"We look brave," said Frog.

"Yes, but are we?"

asked Toad.

Frog and Toad went outside.

"We can try to climb this mountain,"

said Frog. "That should tell us

if we are brave."

Frog went leaping over rocks,

and Toad came puffing up

behind him.

They came to a dark cave.

A big snake came out of the cave.

"Hello lunch," said the snake

when he saw Frog and Toad.

He opened his wide mouth.

Frog and Toad jumped away.

Toad was shaking.

"I am not afraid!" he cried.

They climbed higher,

and they heard a loud noise.

Many large stones

were rolling down the mountain.

"It's an avalanche!" cried Toad.

46

Frog and Toad jumped away.

Frog was trembling.

"I am not afraid!" he shouted.

They came to the top

of the mountain.

The shadow of a hawk

fell over them.

Frog and Toad

jumped under a rock.

The hawk flew away.

"We are not afraid!"

screamed Frog and Toad

at the same time.

Then they ran down the mountain

very fast.

They ran past the place

where they saw the avalanche.

They ran past the place

where they saw the snake.

They ran all the way

to Toad's house.

"Frog, I am glad to have

a brave friend like you," said Toad.

He jumped into the bed

and pulled the covers

over his head.

"And I am happy to know

a brave person like you, Toad,"

said Frog.

He jumped into the cupboard

and shut the door.

Toad stayed in the bed,

and Frog stayed in the cupboard.

They stayed there

for a long time,

just feeling very brave together.

## The Dream

Toad was asleep,

and he was having a dream.

He was on a stage,

and he was wearing

a costume.

Toad looked out

into the dark.

Frog was sitting

in the theatre.

A strange voice from far away said,

"PRESENTING THE GREATEST TOAD

IN ALL THE WORLD!"

Toad took a deep bow.

Frog looked smaller

as he shouted,

"Hooray for Toad!"

"TOAD WILL NOW

PLAY THE PIANO VERY WELL,"

said the strange voice.

Toad played the piano,

and he did not miss a note.

"Frog," cried Toad,

"can you play the piano like this?"

"No," said Frog.

It seemed to Toad

that Frog looked even smaller.

"TOAD WILL NOW WALK

ON A HIGH WIRE,

AND HE WILL NOT FALL DOWN,"

said the voice.

Toad walked on the high wire.

"Frog," cried Toad,

"can you do tricks like this?"

"No," peeped Frog,

who looked very, very small.

"TOAD WILL NOW DANCE,

AND HE WILL BE WONDERFUL,"

said the voice.

58

"Frog, can you be as wonderful

as this?" said Toad

as he danced all over the stage.

There was no answer.

Toad looked out into the theatre.

Frog was so small

that he could not be seen or heard.

"Frog," said Toad,

"where are you?"

There was still no answer.

"Frog, what have I done?"

cried Toad.

Then the voice said,

"THE GREATEST TOAD WILL NOW..."

"Be quiet!" screamed Toad.

"Frog, Frog, where have you gone?"

Toad was spinning in the dark.

"Come back, Frog," he shouted.

"I will be lonely!"

"I am here," said Frog.

Frog was standing near Toad's bed.

"Wake up, Toad," he said.

"Frog, is that really you?" said Toad.

"Of course it is me," said Frog.

"And are you

your own right size?" asked Toad.

62

"Yes, I think so," said Frog.

Toad looked at the sunshine

coming through the window.

"Frog," he said,

"I am so glad

that you came over."

"I always do," said Frog.

Then Frog and Toad

ate a big breakfast.

And after that

they spent a fine, long day together.